Published by Two Lions, New York
www.apub.com

Amazon, the Amazon logo, and Two Lions are trademarks of Amazon.com, Inc., or its affiliates.

ISBN-13: 9781542042635 (hardcover) | ISBN-10: 1542042631 (hardcover)

The illustrations are rendered in digital media.
Book design by Abby Dening

Printed in China | First Edition
1 3 5 7 9 10 8 6 4 2

To my great nephew, Samuel Ari Seltzer;
his parents, Justin and Lauren;
and Ricco
—E. S.

For a cute little rabbit called Barth
—R. G.

To start the day, we lift a limping Edgar Elephant with our **Rescue Rabbits Super-Excavator.**

Next we help fifty sick hippos feel all better.

And then we block traffic in our **Rescue Rabbits Limo**
to help the Duckling family cross the road.

Then we whiz to our next rescue on our **Rescue Rabbits Super-Skis.**

Kevin Kangaroo is hungry but hasn't caught one fish all day. He is also seasick and has a rash. We feed him oatmeal and put our **Rescue Rabbits Rash-Away Lotion** on his rash because . . .

we are **THE RESCUE RABBITS**.

It's been a busy day, but it's not over yet.
We head back to **Rescue Rabbits Headquarters**.
This is where we get news about critters in trouble.

We're just getting settled in our seats when suddenly . . .

Rex has ants in his royal pants and chopsticks up his royal nose, AND he's stuck up a tree.

How did this happen?

Rex tells us everything.
How he used his mama's
chopsticks to break
the glass around
her ant farm.

He just wanted to see
what would happen.

How his mama
screamed when she
saw what he did.

First we have to find him!
The GPS on our **Special-Ops Telephone**
isn't sending us the correct location.

Then Chip jumps in with his brand-new **Rescue Rabbits Tracking Device** and finds Rex in minutes.

Way to go, Chip!

Finally, we're on the scene! Spot and Chip hose down his royal pants with our all-organic **Rescue Rabbits ANT-BE-GONE Foaming Spray.**

Dot and Ace blow his royal nose
with our **Rescue Rabbits
Monogrammed Hankies.**

HO

Now Prince Rex is both ant- and chopstick-free, but he is still stuck up a tree.

We bring a ladder from our **Rescue Rabbits Super-Truck Z100**, but Prince Rex says he does not climb ladders.

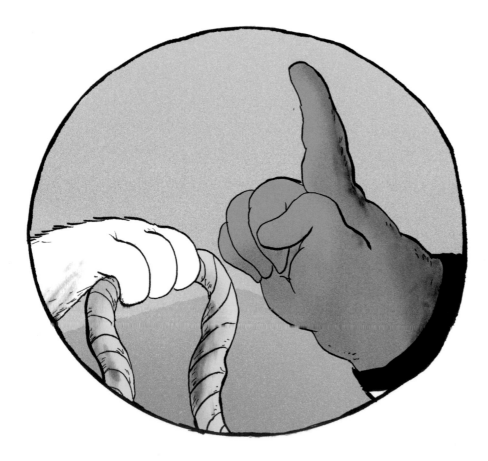

We bring a rope from our **Rescue Rabbits Super-Chopper 9000**, but Prince Rex says he does not climb ropes.

Our tools and gadgets won't solve this problem. We need a new plan. So we do a **Rescue Rabbits Huddle**.

Then we get a BIG idea. . . .

We bring Queen Rex,
the prince's mama,
in our **Rescue Rabbits
Super-Chopper 9000.**

BANG!

But then Dot climbs out and locates the problem.

She gets the chopper humming again.

We've reached the prince! The queen demands that Rex come down this instant. But nobody can hear her. Then Spot takes out our **Rescue Rabbits Super-Megaphone**.

GET DOWN THIS INSTANT!!!

Now everyone can hear just fine.

Prince Rex gets down.
He approaches the queen.

I'm sorry
I broke your
ant farm,
Mama.

We hold our breath
to see what the queen
will do. . . .

It's okay. I never liked those silly ants anyway.

She opens her arms to hug the prince!

We do our
**Rescue Rabbits
Happy Dance**
to celebrate because . . .